Doreen Cronin · Scott Menchin

RESCUE BUNNIES

Balzer + Bray

An Imprint of HarperCollins Publishers

For First Responders everywhere
—D.C.

For Robert Stanley Menchin
—S.M.

Balzer + Bray is an imprint of HarperCollins Publishers.

Rescue Bunnies
Text copyright © 2010 by Doreen Cronin
Illustrations copyright © 2010 by Scott Menchin
All rights reserved. Manufactured in China.
No part of this book may be used or reproduced in any manner whatsoever without written
permission except in the case of brief quotations embodied in critical articles and reviews.
For information address HarperCollins Children's Books, a division of HarperCollins Publishers,
10 East 53rd Street, New York, NY 10022.
www.harpercollinschildrens.com

Library of Congress Cataloging-in-Publication Data
Cronin, Doreen.
    Rescue Bunnies / by Doreen Cronin ; illustrated by Scott Menchin. — 1st ed.
        p.   cm.
    Summary: Newbie struggles to pass her field test to become a full-fledged Rescue Bunny.
    ISBN 978-0-06-112871-4 (trade bdg.) — ISBN 978-0-06-112872-1 (lib. bdg.)
    [1. Rabbits—Fiction.   2. Giraffe—Fiction.   3. Rescue work—Fiction.   4. Humorous stories.]
    I. Menchin, Scott, ill.   II. Title.
PZ7.C88135Re   2010   2009030835
[E]—dc22   CIP
                                                                                                  AC

Typography by Carla Weise
10 11 12 13 14 SCP 10 9 8 7 6 5 4 3 2 1
❖
First Edition

Newbie is a Rescue Bunny trainee.

She has passed the
Physical Fitness Test.

She has passed
the Emergency Rescue
Roping Test.

She has even passed
the Blind Taste Test.

The last test will be the toughest
of all . . . the Field Test.
 Until then her job is to alphabetize
the spice rack.

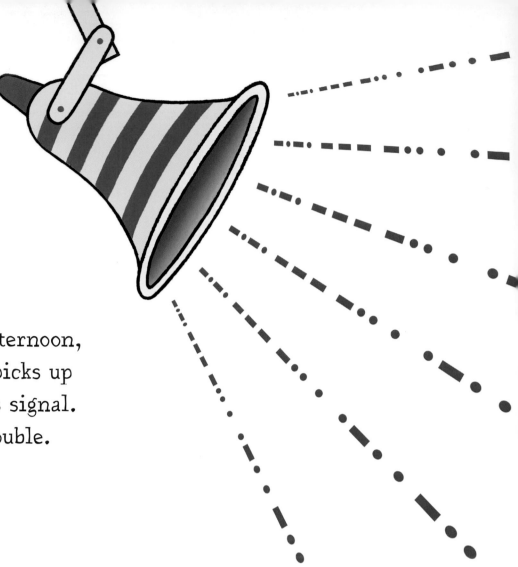

Late Tuesday afternoon,
the second shift picks up
an urgent distress signal.
A giraffe is in trouble.

"Newbie!" shouts the chief.
"Grab your pack—today is your
Field Test!"

Unfortunately, Newbie has tied
herself to the spice rack with a
double figure-eight rescue knot.
"Get the kid off the spice rack!"
yells the chief.

Finally, the Field Test!
"We're headed to hyena country,"
warns the chief. "If they get too close,
it's a Code Red."

"What's a Code Red?" asks Newbie.
"Evacuation," replies Bunny 1.
"What happens to the giraffe?"
asks Newbie.
"You want the truth?" asks Bunny 1.

You can't handle the truth!

"We leave, giraffe stays," answers Bunny 1.

The giraffe is in sight and the drop zone is clear.

"Watch out for the tree, kid," warns the chief.

Ouch.

Uh-oh.

I'm okay!

The Rescue Bunnies are on the scene.
Chief gives his orders:

Secure the area!

Check for injuries!

Don't trip on the rope, kid!

The bunnies examine the giraffe for injuries.

"You missed those giant bumps on her head," announces Newbie.

"They're called horns, kid," says the chief.

Bunny 1 scans the savanna with his binoculars.
"HYENAS ON THE HORIZON!"

"Hyenas?" repeats Newbie.

The Rescue Bunnies race against the clock.
They try to dig the giraffe out. She won't budge.

They try to push her out.
She won't budge.

The bunnies devise a complex system of cables and pulleys.

She budges just a bit . . . and then sinks back in.

"What can I do to help, Chief?" Newbie asks.

"Babysit the giraffe," replies the chief as he walks away.

"Why do I get stuck with the giraffe?" asks Newbie.

"Why do I get stuck with the trainee?" asks the giraffe.

"It's my first day out here," says the giraffe.

"Me too," says Newbie.

"I'm scared," whispers the giraffe.

"I'll hold your . . . ear," answers Newbie.

"Works for me," says the giraffe.

"What's a Code Red?" asks the giraffe.
"Do you want the truth?" says Newbie.
"I think so," answers the giraffe.
Newbie hesitates. "We evacuate."
"What happens to me?" asks the giraffe.
"Well . . ."

The hyenas are moving in.

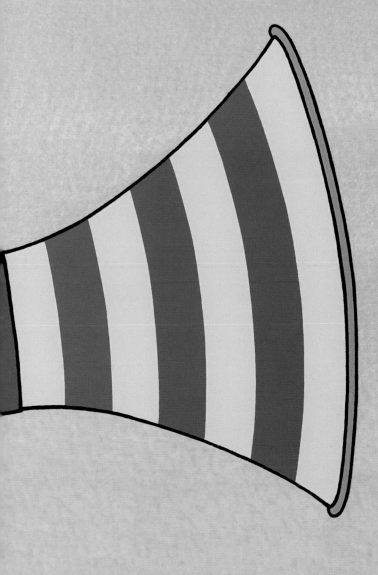

"CODE RED!"

yells the chief.

Newbie doesn't care about her
Field Test anymore.
She ties herself to the giraffe
with a double figure-eight
rescue knot.

"I'M NOT LEAVING HERE
WITHOUT THE GIRAFFE!"

"Crazy kid," mutters the chief.
He turns to the crew.

"Grab the kid's feet!"
yells the chief.
   One by one, the bunnies
form a rescue chain.

"Two steps to the left!"
"Two steps to the right!"
"Move up!"
"Move back!"

"Forward one, two,

THREE!"

It's not the first time the Bunny Hop has dragged someone out of the mud.

The ride back to the command center is quiet.

"I guess I didn't pass the Field Test, huh, Chief?" says Newbie.

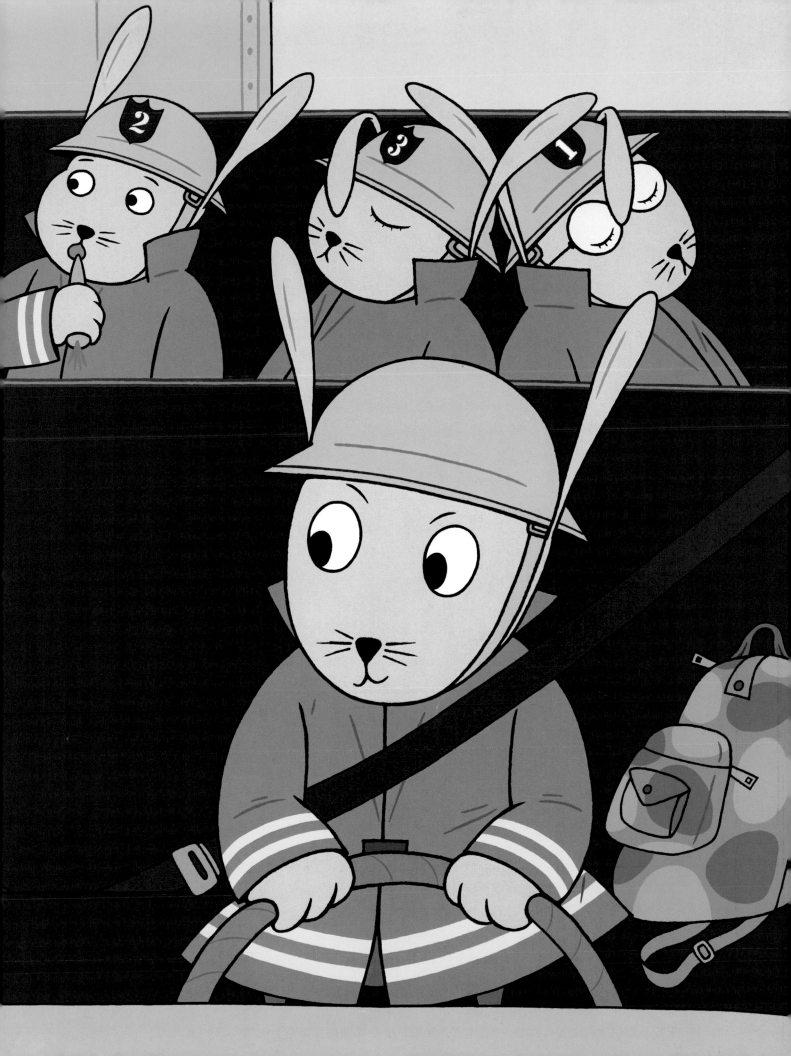

The chief puts his arm around Newbie.
"You've got a lot of heart, kid," he says.
"The rest—you can learn."